THE CLOCKWORK ICE DRAGON

A STEAMPUNK CHRISTMAS NOVELLA

LIZ DELTON

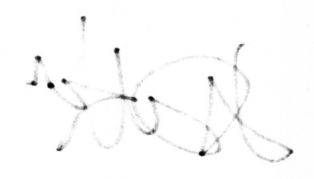

The Clockwork Ice Dragon
A Steampunk Christmas Novella
Liz Delton

ISBN 978-1-7345231-7-1

Tourmaline & Quartz Publishing
P. O. Box 193, North Granby, CT 06060

ONE

FOUR DAYS UNTIL CHRISTMAS

The snow began as Aurelia Sundon switched off all the gas lamps in her workshop, except the one over her drafting table. She paused at the window when she spotted the delicate white snowflakes drifting down from the dark sky.

They were the first snowflakes she had ever seen in her life.

Wide-eyed, she watched them drift onto the street below as she gnawed on the end of her pencil. She couldn't go outside and see them in person. Not yet.

However much she wanted to feel the snow on her face, she had work to do. She put her hand on the cold glass, seeing at once the drifting snowflakes and her pale reflection, her short dark hair that barely hid her ears and her curved button nose. She shivered, then took her hand off the glass, leaving a foggy imprint of her hand there. *How had it gotten cold enough to snow?* She had read nothing about this amazing winter phenomenon in the papers.

Shaking her head, she perched herself on her creaky stool, then sifted through the scraps of paper on her drafting table, each with a fragment of an idea on it that she had scribbled in her spare moments.

She was running out of time to finish her plans for her magnetic train. The City of Soldark's Magistrate of Invention had announced just two days ago that they would be open for submissions from non-union inventors, but only on Christmas Day. It was a once-in-a-lifetime chance. Why they picked Christmas of all days, Aurelia couldn't fathom, but ever since she had learned the news, she had started formulating her plan. She only had four days left.

Her mag-train would win the attention of the magistrate. It had to. It would revolutionize transportation from Soldark into the surrounding countryside, neighboring cities, and even the countries Aurelia had only heard of but never seen. Only people who could afford airship fare could ever get the chance to see the world outside of Soldark. She just had trouble finding enough time to put her dream onto paper and into metal.

Four days to create a working prototype. She crumpled up another botched drawing and tossed it on the floor, where it landed among the stacks of sheet metal, iron molds, her precious magnets, and spools of copper wiring. She gazed out at the snow, falling like bits of stuffing past her window. She still couldn't allow herself to stop working to go out and see it.

Just like her chance with the Magistrate of Invention, the snow was an extraordinary occurrence here in Soldark. Rather sensibly, she told herself, she would focus on her train, instead. At least she could watch the snow from the window.

She cursed her boss, Mr. Augur, at the metal foundry. Even though he knew she was submitting something to the Magistrate of Invention, he had been scheduling her for twelve-hour days all week. The only time she had for her project was when she *should* be catching up on sleep. But as always, she needed the money, so she couldn't pass up the work. Obviously, Mr. Augur didn't want to lose her. If she made it into the inventor's union, all kinds of job opportunities would open up for her. Better paying ones.

Aurelia sketched long into the night, occasionally glancing out her window to watch the snow piling up outside on the street. *Soon*, she kept promising herself, she would go out and see the snow. Soon, she would have a viable plan.

She couldn't see very well with just the one lamp, but she couldn't afford to keep all of the lights on all night. She could barely afford the rent on her workshop as it was. Most of her foundry wages went to her parents' house on the outskirts of the city, where her parents were trying desperately to keep their farm from falling into the ground—literally. Two months ago, the chicken coop had collapsed after a storm, and repairing it hadn't been cheap. If her parents lost the farm, they would have to move into the city, and it was likely that Aurelia would have to give up her workshop to make ends meet, and that would be the end of her inventing dreams.

Most nights when Aurelia worked too late—and tonight was looking like one of those nights—she would curl up on the cot she kept folded up under her drafting table. The few trains into the country didn't run past midnight. But she could change that.

The drawing was taking shape. She had already worked out the schematics in her head during the long hours at the foundry, and scribbled bits and pieces of the design—as she thought of them—onto scraps of paper she stuffed into her pockets. And she had even done some preliminary work on the train itself. She reached for the

❄ 4

compass out of her pencil cup, telling herself she could go out and see the snow once she added the final touch: the wheels.

Of course, the idea of the mag-train was that it didn't need wheels; it would hover over the track. But by a stroke of incredible luck, she had acquired an old early-model steam train at a scrap metal auction several months back, and it had the most gorgeous wheels. The antique steam train had inspired her dream of the mag-train in the first place.

After she had stored it in her parents' barn, she had spent days combing it for parts she could repurpose or sell. At first, that's all it was to her: a hunk of parts. But as she inspected it, she realized it was in pretty good shape for an antique that had sat in an auction yard for a few decades. And even though the wheels were heavy and would add unnecessary weight to the levitating train, the spokes were pristine, the bolts well-seated, and the treads suited to magnetizing. They would add flare if nothing else.

Eventually she realized the wheels would be the key to her invention. If she could use the same tracks as the steam trains, there would be no reason for the city of Soldark not to use her mag-train. It would be faster, and less likely to break down or need parts, and the best part was, since the wheels would levitate off the tracks, rain and dust and grime wouldn't affect them. *And snow*, she thought suddenly, tearing her gaze away from her design.

It was still snowing. She stood up and stretched, then gave her design one last glance: it was finished. There was only one hitch in her plan. She still needed the electricity.

She grabbed her coat off its peg by the door, and slipped out of her workshop, locking it behind her with a big brass key. She crept down the wooden staircase, careful to walk quietly past the other tenants' doors. Some, like her, slept nights in their shops, either because they were hard at work or just didn't have a home to go to. Not many who rented in this part of Soldark were lucky enough to be part of the inventor's union and got by from job to job.

Finally, she eased open the heavy door at the bottom of the stairs, and she breathed in the unfamiliar scent of snow in the night air. Her boots scuffed the pristine white flakes that had already piled up a half-inch or so on the sidewalk, covering up the grime that she knew lay underneath.

She held out her hand and watched as the snow fell on her palm, melting after an instant. She grinned, gazing up at the black night sky, where thousands of snowflakes drifted down toward the earth. She shivered, her forearms warm at least since she hadn't bothered to unlace her leather arm-warmers that kept her forearms free from pencil marks. Her coat was thin, not made for this temperature.

"What do you think?"

She whirled around and came face to face with Frederick Grandville, who rented one of the workshops on the floor beneath hers. He was the son of a wealthy businessman, and although he was quite handsome, Aurelia despised everything about him. She took a step away from him, crossing her arms over her middle as she took in his foppish appearance.

His chestnut hair was ruffled, which was quite unusual for him, and he'd crammed a brown top hat over it—something Aurelia found ridiculous. He was wearing his usual garb: the embroidered waistcoat underneath a fine brown coat, both tailored to fit his form perfectly. His golden eyes watched her keenly, and his mouth quirked up in a tantalizing smile.

"It's wonderful," Aurelia said coldly. She turned to go back inside, her magical moment in the snow dirtied by his pretentious presence.

"Wait, Aurelia," Frederick said, his smooth voice grating her nerves. "Don't leave because of me."

She rolled her eyes, fidgeting with the thin edge of lace poking out of her arm-warmers. "I don't do anything because of you. I need to get back to my workshop. I have plans that need finishing. Excuse me."

He didn't step aside, instead leaned against the door, still in her way. He crossed his arms over his chest, gazing at the snow. "Come on. I know you came out here to look at the snow. So did I. We don't even have to talk."

"Move aside."

"Aurelia," he pleaded, cocking his head and gazing at her under the rim of his top hat. "It's almost Christmas. Can't you be nice to me for once?"

Aurelia took a deep breath, looking up at the majestic sky and the twirling fall of snow. She leaned against the brick building, resolutely looking in the other direction. She *did* want to watch the snow.

"So..." he began.

"I thought you weren't going to talk?"

"Aurelia, come on!" He reached out and wrapped his hands around her forearms. She could almost feel his warmth. "When are you going to let this go? I had no idea I was up against you for the apprenticeship. You and I hadn't even talked in months."

She pulled her arms out of his grasp, and tried to shove past him to the door, but he planted himself in her way. "Why would you?" she scathed. "And once they saw your last name, it didn't matter who else applied for the apprenticeship, did it?" She took a step to her right, and he mirrored her.

His face crumpled. "That's what this is about?" he asked, aghast. "You think they gave it to me because of my father?"

"Of course they did. He owns the whole city." She tried to step to the left this time, but he moved that way too.

"He doesn't own it—he just powers it!"

"Same thing." She gave up trying to get around him and slumped against the brick wall again. *Maybe I can just ignore him,* she thought. *At least until he lets me inside so I can get some sleep before my shift tomorrow.* She stifled a yawn, then shivered. Her coat was really not made for this weather.

"So what do you think?" Frederick asked again, nodding at the falling flakes, as though he were solely responsible for the once-in-a-lifetime snowfall.

"I told you, it's wonderful," she said through grit teeth.

"I thought you'd like it."

"You're really full of yourself, you know that, right?"

He grinned at her, then stuck his hands in the pockets of his waistcoat. "It was very difficult."

"What was?"

"Getting it to snow."

She scoffed. "You didn't."

"I did."

Aurelia looked up to the heavens and breathed, "You're ridiculous. I don't believe you."

"I'll have to show you then. I'll have it back late tonight after its first voyage."

"*It*? What are you talking about?"

Frederick beamed, and Aurelia recognized the smile as one she used to enjoy before he went and betrayed her. She forced herself to look away, clenching her fists.

Words began to tumble out of Frederick's mouth in his excitement. "I told you: I got it to snow. It's my invention—my prototype to show to the inventor's union on Christmas. Did you hear they're accepting plans from non-union inventors?"

Aurelia closed her eyes briefly, trying to wrap her head around the idea that Frederick had made an invention that had made it snow here in Soldark, the place where it was always warm, and the sun shone year-round. Then she said in a near whisper, "Don't you dare. Don't you dare tell me you're submitting a plan to the inventor's union."

His face fell. "What? Why?"

"Why?" she scathed, then lowered her voice as a group of young laborers trotted down the sidewalk on their way to a late shift—or early shift, Aurelia had completely lost track of the time. "You've got an apprenticeship at

Penydarren Place; you'll be able to get into the union in less than a year, guaranteed. What are you doing submitting plans now? Are you planning on ruining my submission for this too?"

"Ruining—What? What are you talking about?"

She threw her hands up. "I'm done talking to you Grandville. Step aside."

Frederick, mouth agape in confusion, didn't try to stop her as she shoved her way to the door.

"What am I talking about indeed," she muttered to herself once the door shut, drawing into the dim stairwell. She glanced back at Frederick through the glass paneled door. He was looking up at the snow falling from the sky. He muttered something to himself and then stalked off down the street, probably to drive home in his top-of-the-line motorcar he kept parked around the corner.

Aurelia scoffed then began trudging back up the staircase, making sure to give Frederick's workshop door a mean look as well, just to vent her feelings some more.

She curled up on the cot in her workshop, underneath a large sheet of canvas she had pulled off one of her train models. She couldn't even smell the oil on it, a scent which permeated the workshop anyway. She turned to watch the snow falling outside her window and drifted to sleep.

TWO

THREE DAYS UNTIL CHRISTMAS

It was still snowing the next morning.

An irritating buzz awoke Aurelia before dawn, the sound of the alarm she had rigged herself. She flung her hand out to stop it, groping around the edge of the drafting table above her. Finally, she laid her hand on the small contraption and flipped the switch over.

She shivered as she pulled back the canvas sheet. At least, she knew she would warm up at the foundry.

Twenty minutes later, she trudged down the lane through the thickening snow. She was glad for the black lace-up boots she wore; the snow had piled up to her ankles already. She didn't have anything warmer to wear than her usual nondescript brown trousers, long-sleeve burgundy undershirt, and brown leather vest. The brown coat was thin but better than nothing.

She thought back to her encounter with Frederick last night and scoffed, her breath clouding the air before her face. As if he knew enough to invent something that could create this. He was a hack, riding along his father's coattails, and always would be.

It snowed in plenty of places in the Galderon Republic, just never here in Soldark, the largest city at the heart of the solarbelt, where it was always sunny and warm. Aurelia didn't know how anyone lived with this freezing precipitation all the time like they did outside the solarbelt. She brushed some snowflakes out of her hair and her fingers came back glittering. It *was* pretty, though.

An intoxicatingly warm scent of hot coffee came over her at the next corner, where Max had parked his newsstand. She had known Max for a few years now, ever since she began renting her workshop space in the Brassborough neighborhood. He had given up the dream years ago of becoming a full-fledged inventor himself, so he ran a newsstand instead. And it wasn't just any newsstand.

Before Aurelia had met him, Max had crafted a first-class wheeled contraption that could hardly even be called a newsstand, it had so many bells and whistles on it—literally. There were bells and whistles at the front for when Max led the steam-powered cart down the street, to park at the next desirable corner. It would follow behind him all by itself as he gave it directions with an enormous control box that he kept slung by his side at all times.

In addition to its uncanny mobility, there were all kinds of compartments on the sides that opened up to display the day's papers—under glass, where a customer could press a button for their desired paper, and a chute would open up and provide them a freshly rolled-up copy. There was a variety of paperbacks for workers to tuck in their back pockets to read during breaks, and an array of snacks and drinks, all in their neat compartments. But today, he had hot coffee.

Aurelia drifted her way over to the newsstand behind some enthusiastic customers admiring Max's newest addition. He had rigged up an enormous metal urn to the corner of the cart, hot steam billowing from it and melting snowflakes on impact. Aurelia watched a customer hand over a copper coin, and Max took a paper cup from where he stood inside the cart, then placed it in a mechanical arm. He flipped a switch and the arm brought the cup over to the urn at the corner and began to fill it with hot coffee.

Impressed, Aurelia smiled at Max and glanced at the newspaper headlines behind glass as she waited her turn. *First Snow in Soldark in over 100 Years Baffles*

Weatherologists. SNOW, is it Good or Bad for Soldark? Aurelia snorted.

"May I try a coffee please?" she asked when she got to the front of the line.

Max grinned at her. "Anything for my favorite inventor!" He inserted a paper cup into the mechanical arm and leaned his elbows on the tiny counter he stood behind. He adjusted his newsie cap, revealing short-cropped hair nearly the same color as his copper skin, which had faint lines around his eyes and mouth because he smiled so often.

"When did you do all this?" she asked in wonder, watching the mechanical arm up close. There were pistons and rods to make up the arm, with a clamp of sorts to hold the cup. What she couldn't figure out was how the urn began to pour coffee into the cup as soon as the cup was underneath the spout.

"Last night," Max said, shrugging. "Couldn't sleep, thought coffee would be a hit seller, and I was right."

Aurelia glanced back at the line forming behind her. He handed her the hot cup and her change. "And I thought *I* was up late," she said, breathing in the warm scent of the coffee. It was a rare treat; she didn't have too many coppers to spare even on paydays, and the cafes and eateries normally charged exorbitant amounts for the beverage.

"Working on your secret project again?" he asked, waggling his eyebrows at her.

A wide grin came across her face. "I finished all the calculations last night. Now I just need to find a power source."

Max scratched his stubbly chin. "And you won't ask—"

"Never. I can find someone other than the Grandvilles to ask for a handout." She huffed, her breath coming out in a cloud of steam. "I better get out of your line," she said, deciding not to tell him about her encounter with Frederick last night. She didn't feel the need to relive the experience.

"All right." Max shrugged. "But if it's going to cost you getting into the inventor's union, you might want to think about swallowing that pride of yours."

She glared at him over her steaming coffee cup. "What pride?" she said, chuckling. "I can get into the union all by myself, you watch me."

"I can't wait to see it in the papers," he replied, tipping his cap to her as she walked away.

THREE

After her twelve-hour shift at the foundry, Aurelia went straight to the train station. She counted out her coppers and saw she had enough for three trips to her parents' farm and back. After that, she'd have to wait until payday, and that wasn't until after Christmas. Mr. Augur had told them this morning that he wouldn't be providing any Christmas bonuses this year and wouldn't even pay them in advance before the holiday.

Not that Aurelia had complained out loud at the news. She could scrape by until after the holiday. Normally, when she ran out of money for train tickets, she'd just sleep in her workshop instead of going home for the night. But now it was just a matter of getting her train completed in time before the Magistrate of Invention sent out judges. She still couldn't believe they were doing it on Christmas Day.

She stepped onto the steam train, harried by the persistent snowflakes. It hadn't let up all day. While she had helped haul and pour giant vats of molten metal all day, she caught glimpses of it through the windows far up on the high walls of the foundry warehouse. She rolled her eyes again as she thought of what Frederick had said last night about the snow. It was just some fluke, some Christmas miracle like you read about in those two-penny paperbacks Max sold at his newsstand.

Normally, she hated taking the train right after her shift got out, when it was packed to the brim with workers heading outside the city, but she needed to get some measurements of the antique train before she brought over all her supplies and tools from the workshop. She wished her workshop were big enough, and that she had the means to bring the train there. It would make this fanciful Christmas deadline a little easier to meet. But she was lucky to even have her second-floor space at all.

As the train squealed to a stop at the small platform just outside city limits, Aurelia squeezed herself between the crush of commuters heading home and emerged onto the platform. The sun-beaten wooden planks of the platform were completely hidden by several inches of snow, and she had to brush off the wrought-iron railing as she descended. Luckily, her parents' farm was only a short walk from here, located in one of the older rural areas that the city hadn't had a chance to develop yet.

She nodded to the man in the small ticket booth at the bottom of the stairs, papers and paraphernalia stacked unceremoniously on wooden ledges behind the counter, a poor comparison to Max's remarkable newsstand. She wished she could have brought her parents some of Max's hot coffee, but she didn't know where his stand might have been after her shift, since he moved around throughout the day.

So she tromped through the snow down the country lane, a leather satchel at her side filled with her notebooks, blueprints, measuring tapes, rulers, and levels. She didn't appreciate the wind whipping snowflakes at her as it barreled across the Morrison's corn fields, which had long since been picked. She shrugged into her coat and ducked her head, wondering if she could find a hat or something at home for the trip back to the workshop.

Finally, she got some relief from the wind as she reached the edge of her parents' land, where a line of trees on either side of the lane offered some shelter. She wasn't looking forward to making this trip back later when it would be properly dark. Even now, she couldn't see the sun, blocked as it was by the snow and clouds.

Two beams of light came at her from the eerie darkness down the lane, accompanied by the chugging sound of an automobile. She darted to the side of the road before it whizzed by her.

She turned to watch it drive off, skidding a little on the slippery dirt track, but she had no idea whose auto it might have been. Her parents didn't often get visitors. She just hoped that it wasn't the bank again. A week before Christmas was surely not the time to be making house calls to lean on mortgagees behind on payments.

The tire tracks provided an easier path to walk in, and it wasn't long before the huge old farmhouse loomed up out of the snowy gloom. The front porch light flickered, illuminating the covered wrap-around deck that was sagging only a little in front of the door. Lights were on all over the house, in fact, upstairs and downstairs, which she found unusual. Her parents were normally very responsible with the gas, and only lit the rooms they absolutely needed to. Electric lights out in the country were harder to come by, and so gas was still cheaper out here.

She followed the tire tracks, which went nearly up to the door, and then the footprints in the snow, until she reached the warmth and light of the porch. The warm scent of freshly baked bread invited her in, and the heavy door creaked as she entered. She drew a deep breath once she got inside and went straight to the fireplace in the sitting room to the left.

Her hands already warming in front of the fire, she heard her father's voice drift down from upstairs. "Is that you, Aurelia?"

"Yes, I'm in the sitting room!" she called back. "I just came to take some measurements, and then I have to get back to the workshop before the last train goes through."

The stairs creaked as her father descended. She turned to warm her backside as he came into the sitting room. There were dark shadows under his eyes and a frown on his sun-weathered face.

"What's wrong?" she asked. "Who came in the auto?"

Her father sank into an old wingback chair beside the fire. "That was Doctor Abbeysworth. Your mother isn't feeling well again."

"What? I thought that medication the doctor gave her last year was working?" Aurelia took off her leather satchel and sank into the other wingback, her train plans forgotten for the moment.

"It might be the sudden cold," her father said, staring into the flickering flames before him. "That's what the doctor said. Or, well, the shock."

"Shock? What do you mean, shock?"

"Well..." he said, frowning. "The snow. Our crops are

well on their way to dying. They're buried in snow, and they won't survive the temperature much longer."

Aurelia gasped. "All of them?"

"All of them."

She closed her eyes for a moment. She hadn't noticed anything wrong with the fields as she'd trudged down the lane, blocked by the trees as they were. If her parents couldn't harvest and sell their turnips, broccoli, and cabbages at the winter markets, they would be in even more dire straits than they already were.

"Don't mention it to your mother again when she wakes up," he said. "We can't have her worrying, not when she's feeling so poorly. The doctor gave her a dose of something strong before she left and prescribed a higher dose of the daily treatment too."

Aurelia took a deep breath, hearing his words add up in her mental ledger of their predicaments. The crops were a devastating subtraction. The higher dosage, another.

"Do you need help with the measurements?" her father asked, his gray eyes lighting up despite the new shadows underneath them.

She shook her head. "No, you stay inside with Mother. Can I borrow a hat?"

As soon as she reached the barn where her train was stored, she paused against the big open doorframe and caught her breath. She only had an hour to take all the measurements and get back to the train platform before the last train went by. If she missed it, she would have to stay at the farm overnight, and she was planning on doing a lot more work before tomorrow's shift at the foundry.

Suddenly her invention's importance towered over her, much like the enormous antique sitting in the dark barn. If her project was picked by the Magistrate of Invention, not only would she be given inventor's union status, but she would receive the prize being offered up: enough money to buy a new farm or fix up the old one; she'd take either.

But before, it had been something she had *wanted*. Now it was something she needed.

She got to work.

She pulled out her headlamp—several weeks' worth of pay, but worth it—and cranked the gear on the side for a few minutes. A light blared out of the bulb, and she strapped the lamp to her forehead. Even if there were enough lights in the barn to illuminate the train, she wasn't about to waste a whiff of her parents' precious gas.

The headlamp threw the train into view in bits and pieces, making drastic shadows as she moved her head and looked it over. It wasn't an entire train, of course, but the front cab, which contained the conductor's controls and the boiler, and one short car attached behind it that would normally haul coal and water. The only place for a passenger right now was in the driver's cab up front, but she didn't need to show the Magistrate of Invention how it would carry passengers. She only needed to show them that it worked.

And once she finished rigging up all the new parts to the train, all she needed was power.

But the amount she would need was exponential and couldn't be generated by the train's boiler alone. She would just have to figure it out while she installed the new parts.

Her beam of light focused on the connecting rods down by the wheels. Those, she needed to lock so the wheels wouldn't turn once the train was hovering magnetically above the track. And when the magnets weren't being powered, the train would be able to rest perfectly on the tracks like it did now. She pulled her plans out of her satchel along with a measuring tape.

Next, she focused her beam on the tracks the train sat on, which ran out of the barn and connected to an old Soldark Line that was abandoned years ago. This was the other reason her project was a perfect idea. She already had the tracks—which she had tripped over and played on endlessly as a kid—so she could test out the train easily without interfering with any active tracks. A few years back, she had even rigged up a farm cart to the tracks so her father could carry heavy equipment down to some of the fields that the abandoned line ran past. She had always been fascinated by trains. But that cart moved by ways of pumping a seesaw-like arm by hand.

She was glad she had already installed the magnets on the tracks a few weeks ago, since now the tracks outside were getting covered in snow. But a little snow wouldn't stop it from levitating, and she did at least have the short length of track inside the barn that was clear. It was certainly enough to experiment on.

She brushed her hand over the frontmost wheel, then yanked it back, burned by the cold. She brought her fingers before her mouth and breathed on them. For a second, she thought of going back inside the house to get a pair of gardening gloves, but hoped she wouldn't be out here long enough to warrant them. Her heavy-duty leather work gloves were back in her workshop in the city. She would have to remember to bring them when she came back tomorrow. If it was still cold and snowing, that is. It was strange not seeing the sun, and even more, she missed the warmth.

Her mother was still sleeping when Aurelia went back inside the house. Aurelia tiptoed over to her bed and gave her a kiss on the forehead before leaving. She tried not to think of how clammy and feverish her mother's forehead felt as she headed back down the creaky stairs, but surely the doctor's new medicine would help. It had the last time.

"Here," her father said, coming out of the sitting room with a pair of gardening gloves, a slouchy hat that might have once been gray, and a swath of burgundy velvet she could use as a scarf. Aurelia thought the velvet might have been a decorative drape from across the back of one of the chairs, but it was warm and soft, and she didn't care.

"Thanks," she said, putting it all on. "I-I'm sorry about the vegetables," she told her father. His gray eyes darted away for a second, then locked back on hers.

"It's certainly not your fault," he said, the sun-kissed wrinkles around his eyes deepening. He straightened his gray button-up shirt—about as dressed up as her father ever got, probably for the doctor's sake—and cleared his throat. "We'll be fine. Everyone will be fine."

She nodded, her throat constricting as she thought of her mother in bed upstairs and the crops dying outside. "I should get back to the workshop. This train isn't going to win in the state it's in right now."

A smile warmed her father's face, and he flicked the tip of her cap. "That's the spirit I want to hear. You'll do wonders as a union inventor."

"All I really want is the prize," she admitted.

He shrugged. "That wouldn't hurt, but with union status, you'll be well employed for the rest of your life."

She smiled. "I better hurry. I'm definitely not walking back to the city in this weather."

FOUR

As she rode the last train back to Soldark, Aurelia leaned heavily on the brass armrest beside her, worrying about her parents, the farm, and her invention. Her foot beat out a ceaseless rhythm, crossed at the ankle over her knee. It was as if she had drunk another jolt of Max's coffee; she was so wired, despite the approach of midnight and the pleasant but normally soporific dim lights in the nearly empty train car.

There was no way now she could think of asking her father to borrow any coppers for train tickets, so she only had two trips she could take to the farm and back. And one of them would be to meet the judge on Christmas Day. She would have to make all of her adjustments in one night, since the next few days leading up to Christmas she was working twelve-hour shifts at the foundry. By a stroke of luck—certainly not out of her boss's good nature—she would have the days between Christmas and the Dawn of the New Year off. It would be a wonderful time to rest. But it taunted her that she had so much free time to look forward to once the judging was over. If only she had as much time leading up to the Magistrate of Invention's deadline.

But she had to make it work, not just for her own sake, but her parents'. If they lost the farm, they'd have to move to the city, and her father would get stuck working in a factory just like Aurelia—but she was young, she didn't mind the back-breaking labor. Her father had run the farm since his own father had willed it to him, sure, but farm work was different. Soldark's factories were run by tyrannous overseers who barely let their workers take breaks and were more concerned about output than safety. Aurelia was careful at the foundry, but who knows what kind of job her father would secure—if he were even able to get one?

And her mother... She sighed as she watched the huge snowflakes speed past outside in the dark, illuminated only by the train's lamp.

Her mother had been doing poorly ever since last year. But Doctor Abbeysworth had prescribed her some morphine and another concoction that seemed to make the condition improve. Aurelia hoped it wasn't this blasted cold that had sunken both her mother's health, and the profits of the farm all in one go.

When she got back to the Brassborough neighborhood, the snow had piled up halfway to her knees. It had been wonderful at first, but when was it going to stop? The city was having a hard time clearing it off the streets and sidewalks, she had read in someone's discarded *Soldark Afternoon Times* on her ten-minute lunch break that afternoon. The automobiles couldn't even pass down most streets without skidding, and there had been a record number of accidents.

She had to yank hard on the door open to the stairs that led up to her workshop. The door carved a flat arcing path in the snow that had piled up in front of the stoop. She shook herself once she was indoors, brushing the snow out of her hair and off her borrowed scarf.

As she began to climb up to her second-floor workshop, her stomach dropped unpleasantly, as if she had missed a step. The lights were on in Frederick Grandville's workshop, she could see them shining brightly through the wavy glass window on his door.

She narrowed her eyes at the perfect little brass sign he had mounted beside the doorframe, *Frederick Grandville the Third, Inventor*. She stared at it for a moment, her eyes boring into the little screws holding the sign in place, her gut churning.

She couldn't ask him.

But she needed power. She only had three days until Christmas, when the judge would meet her at the farm. And the last thing in the republic she wanted other than embarrassing herself as a failed inventor, was to let down her parents now. She let out an irritated breath and put her hand on the doorknob.

It turned on its own, and she jumped back.

Frederick stood in the doorway, just as shocked as she was. She pretended to adjust her scarf as she mounted the next stair.

"Aurelia," he said, reaching out to try and catch her arm. She grabbed for the unreliable railing instead. "I've been waiting for you all night. I have to talk to you."

Her heart thudded. The words *I have to talk to you too,* burned her tongue, but she didn't say them.

"Something's wrong," he blurted, tucking his hands into the pockets of his blue and silver brocade waistcoat. For the first time, she recognized the manic look on his face. His eyes were darting all around, and his hair was ruffled as if he had been running his hands through it.

She took another step up, facing him. "What?"

He glanced through the foggy glass window leading

outside, and said, "It won't stop."

"What won't stop?" she asked, becoming annoyed. She had work to do, cutting electrical wire and packing up the electromagnets to bring back to the farm. If she wasn't going to ask him now, she needed to get some work done before catching a few hours' sleep.

"It won't stop snowing."

"Well, yes, I noticed," she said. "It's a little inconvenient, but it's fairly nice for the season anyway. What, are you worried you'll be snowed in here and can't get home to the family estate?"

"No," he said, reaching out and grabbing her arm with both hands. "It's not that. I told you—I made it snow. And it won't stop."

Aurelia pulled away from him and flung her hands up in exasperation. "What in the sun-drenched republic are you talking about? I thought you were just joking about making it snow."

He shook his head. "It's my invention for Christmas Day. I did a test run last night, when you and I met outside. But it was supposed to come back. It didn't come back."

"What didn't come back?"

"The clockwork ice dragon."

FIVE

Aurelia insisted Frederick come up to her second-floor workshop and explain while she got down to work. As she compared her new measurements to her blueprints, he told her about his invention.

"You converted an airship into something to make it snow?" she clarified for perhaps the third time. "And you made it look like a dragon?"

"Yes," he admitted. "The gears at the base of the wings actually help power—"

"And it's stuck up there right now?" she interrupted around the pencil in her mouth as she stared at the blueprints. She tweaked one of the numbers, neatly crossing off her original calculation.

"Yes, and it won't respond to the emergency return

signal I worked into it," he said. "It was supposed to come back after the test last night—three hours. I've tried boosting the signal, but it's still up there, churning up the clouds and dropping the temperature."

The pencil fell from Aurelia's mouth and clattered across the floor as the realization came to her.

"You!" she pointed a finger at him as she advanced upon him. She stopped half-way when she almost ran into a stack of crates holding her magnets. "You're the reason my parents' crops are dead! The reason my mother's health suddenly declined! And you thought you could just do whatever you wanted to the weather?"

The finger she was still pointing at him was shaking. She lowered it.

"I...Aurelia, I'm so sorry. Is your mother all right? I didn't know."

Her chest tightened, and she didn't reply, afraid her words would come out high-pitched and pitiful. She turned around and grabbed a spool of wire, then stuffed it into a crate of magnets. Her wire-cutters were next. Then her toolbelt.

"I didn't know," Frederick said softly, placing a hand on her arm.

She pulled away. "Don't touch me, Grandville. I should go to the police right now and report you for meddling with the weather and causing so many catastrophes. Have you even read the papers? Seen how many automobile accidents there've been?"

"Please, I need your help."

"Help?" She scoffed. "Why would I ever help you? Why don't you just go to your father and ask him to help you out of this mess?"

"I can't," he said in a strangled sort of voice. "No one will help me."

"What about your friends at the Arts Bank Club, you know plenty of top inventors."

Frederick seemed to shrink in on himself, and he found a closed crate to sit on. "They're not my real friends. I don't really have any to be honest. They'd probably turn me in faster than you for this invention gone wrong. And none of them know I'm trying to get into the inventor's union this way. They'd resent me for it. They all earned their place through merit, they'd say."

Aurelia fiddled with the toolbelt still in her hands, carefully rolling it up so nothing fell out of its many leather pockets. She hadn't known that. Frederick always seemed surrounded by friends and lackeys, on the rare occasion she ran into him.

"But what about your father?" she asked again. She bent down and stowed the toolbelt in the nearest crate bound for the farm.

His eyes widened. "I can't tell him I made a mistake," he said incredulously.

"Oh, please," she said, turning away and digging through a metal cabinet beside her drafting table. "He thinks the world of you. He'll help you."

"I-I can't ask him."

Aurelia pulled out her torque gun and a container of heavy bolts to go with it, then turned to Frederick. "You didn't tell him you're competing either, did you?"

He dropped his face into his hands and shook his head.

Aurelia wrinkled her face in surprise. She watched him rub his eyes for a moment, and memories of what the two of them used to be like together threatened to wash over her. The way he always asked how her day was—*No*. It was over between them, even before he betrayed her, then stole that apprenticeship from her.

She crossed her arms over her chest. "Fine, I'll help you."

He jerked his head up. "Really?"

"Really. But you are going to do something for me in return."

SIX

TWO DAYS UNTIL CHRISTMAS

After her shift, Aurelia hastily stopped by her workshop to lug all her crates down the stairs and onto a handcart. She pulled the handcart through the snow to the nearest train station. Now gray and dirty, the snow had lost its wonder—mostly because of what had happened to her parents and now because she was going to have to help Frederick when she was supposed to be working on her own invention. The many footprints throughout the day had packed the snow down some, but lugging the handcart over the uneven frozen path wasn't easy.

She barely made it onto the next train and had to shove her way in with the cart, earning many irritated grunts and glances from her fellow passengers. She kept her eyes forward and didn't acknowledge any of them. She breathed in the smell of home from her borrowed scarf, and used her grip on the cart to catch her balance when the train began to move.

Fresh tire tracks led down the lane to her parents' house, making it easier to pull the heavy cart. After switching hands yet again, she finally spotted the porch light in the snowy gloom. She puffed out a sigh of relief and trudged on.

A newer model automobile sat in front of the house, and Aurelia wondered why the doctor was here again. She left the cart out in the snow and rushed up to the front door, her heart racing.

When she opened the door, she came face to face with Frederick.

"Oh, it's you. I thought the doctor—" Aurelia spotted her father over Frederick's shoulder, standing awkwardly in the doorway to the sitting room.

"I'll get that cart for you, Aurelia," Frederick offered.

"No, leave it, it's going to the barn," she said, knowing he was just trying to butter her up since she had agreed to help him.

Frederick dawdled over by the front door instead, fiddling with the pockets of his waistcoat, burgundy and gold today.

Aurelia ignored him and strode over to her father.

"How's Mother doing today?"

Her father gave her a wan smile. "Better. Definitely better. She was awake all day, though, so she went to bed early."

"Good."

"And what's—" Her father began quietly, eyeing Frederick by the door.

"Er...he's helping me power the train."

"Really?" Her father's eyes widened. "What made you change—"

"I'll tell you later. We should probably get to work," she said louder, including Frederick in the conversation. Aurelia squeezed her father's shoulder before heading out the door with Frederick.

Outside in the snow, she grabbed the handle of the cart before Frederick could and wheeled it around his automobile.

"I didn't know you had your own auto," she said, fighting to pull the cart through the deep snow and heading to the barn, a short distance from the right side of the house. Her footsteps from yesterday had already filled in.

"It's not mine. I borrowed it."

She scoffed. "Why can't you just borrow an airship to go get your clockwork ice dragon to come down?"

"I did ask," he said defensively, "but no one will let me take one alone and certainly not in this weather."

"This weather," she muttered incredulously under her breath. "And whose fault is that?"

"I can hear you, you know."

"Good."

"Aurelia, can we just be civil for once? I came to you asking for help because you're a brilliant inventor and a kind person. You can go back to hating me in peace when we're done. We've both had rough patches when we've been there for each other."

Aurelia bristled as they came under the shelter of the barn. "I don't want to talk about any of that. Let's just get to work."

She brought the crates over beside her train and ran a gloved hand lovingly over the front wheel. Success was in sight. She knew it. She would get her power.

"Wait, I thought we were going to figure out how to bring the clockwork dragon down first?" Frederick asked as she pulled out her torque gun and bolts.

"I only have tonight to make the rest of the adjustments before the judging on Christmas. I've barely had any time to work on it since they announced the contest. We can talk while I work."

For a second, he smiled—at some old memory perhaps—then furrowed his brow. "But Aurelia, we have to stop the snow. The city is in a panic. Autos are barely able to move—I was lucky there were some chains in the garage to rig onto my tires to even make it out here. People are freezing, and the crops—"

He stopped talking at her icy glare.

"Well, what do you want me to do?" she asked. "I can secure these bolts while we talk." Already hooked up to the pneumatic line in the barn, she revved the torque gun. It roared as loud as a buzz saw.

She winced. "Ok, I'll just run these wires then."

"What about tomorrow? Can't you work on it then?"

"I can't—I don't have the—tonight's the only night I have. I thought we came here so you could help hook up the electricity?"

"What, do you have a night shift on Christmas Eve or something?" he prodded.

"I can't afford another train ticket!" she burst. "Okay? So can we get on with this?"

His face fell. "Oh. Oh, I'm sorry, I shouldn't have—"

"That's right. you shouldn't have. Did you even bring anything to hook up the electrical? Or was that just another empty promise?"

He tucked his hands in his waistcoat pockets and cleared his throat. "No, I didn't, sorry. I thought we'd figure out the ice dragon tonight, and we could do the train's electrical tomorrow. The snow's only going to keep piling up."

Aurelia rolled her eyes.

He continued, "But-but I can give you train fare or drive you out here tomorrow to finish your invention, even. It's the least I can do for causing you so much grief with this snowstorm."

She let out an exasperated sigh. "Fine. But I'm still running these wires."

Even if she didn't take Frederick's money, maybe she could borrow a few coppers from Max. She could pay him back next week—either with her wages, or, she hoped, the prize money. She hated asking favors from Max, but she didn't really have many other friends.

"So why is it still up there?" she asked, clipping a wire and jerking her head up to the sky. "Hasn't it run out of fuel yet? What's it running on?"

"Well, it's steam and coal powered like the original airship I converted, but the clockwork wings and workings I added allow it to keep operating once it gets going. They recharge it, in a way, with their movement."

"And you think you rigged the timer wrong to come back?"

"I must have," he said, shrugging.

She nodded. He was remarkably unashamed of his failure, at least to her, anyway. She was sure his father

❄ 42

could have figured out a solution with all his resources at Grandville Electric. But she did understand Frederick's desire to remain anonymous about creating this devastating storm. The papers would drag him—and his father's company—through the mud if they ever found out who caused it.

"The clockwork... it's run with electricity generated by the steam engine?"

"Yes, that's the problem. If it were only steam powered, it would have run out of fuel by now."

She nodded again, looking down at the wire in her hands, her thoughts churning. "The train I'm working on is going to channel a lot of electrical energy through the magnets in order to make the train levitate off the tracks. I wonder... Have you ever heard of an electromagnetic pulse?"

His eyes widened. "Yes," he said slowly. "If we could even pull it off, wouldn't it short out everything powered by electricity in all of Soldark?"

She shrugged, then climbed up into the train cab with her measured wire pieces in hand. She hoisted herself into the conductor's cab and pulled open the control panel she had already begun work on a few weeks ago. "It would depend on the force of the pulse, but it would short some things, I'm sure. Wouldn't that be an acceptable trade to get this snow to stop?"

"But we might get discovered that way—I mean, *I* might get discovered," he corrected, seeing her sharp glare as she looked up from the control panel, wire cutters in hand.

With everything hooked up to the panel, she began to run the wires carefully inside the cabin. It didn't need to look too pretty for the test run, but she didn't want the judge tripping on them or anything. She began to bundle them along one wall, tucking them around the large bolts that secured outer panels and windows.

"So, do you know how to make an electromagnetic pulse or what?" Frederick demanded, poking his head into the cab.

She smiled where she crouched, tucking the ends of the wires through a small hole that led outside, where they would connect to the coal cart. "Maybe."

"Let's get on with it! Maybe the city won't care if they lose power for a short time, if this abominable storm stops. They might not even figure out it was me. And half of Soldark still runs gas lamps and heat anyway."

"I know how to make it happen," she said, still trying to jam the wires into the small hole she had drilled a while back, "but I don't think we should leave the radius of the thing up to chance. Having the pulse wide enough to reach the ice dragon might shut down *the whole city*,

Frederick. I know dumping snow on all those poor people wasn't a problem for you, but—"

"I didn't mean for it to be this much!" He lurched up the steep steps into the cab, coming too close to her. "Let me help you with that."

"Fine," she snapped, dodging around him and getting out of the cab, clinging to the handle as she practically leapt to the ground. "Pass them through and I'll pull from the other side."

He passed her one wire at a time, and she pulled them as far as they could comfortably go, leaving a nice gap over the connector between cars. She began to connect them to the secondary panel in the coal car.

"I want to find a way to focus the pulse, if we're going to do this," she said.

"And then we can use it to stop the ice dragon?"

"Yes. I accidentally stumbled across the pulse when I made the miniature prototype for the train. Shorted everything in my workshop and actually fried a few things permanently. That's why we can't just let it go off and possibly affect the whole city. Entire electrical systems and units could be permanently damaged. And your father's company..." she trailed off, knowing that would convince him.

"Huh," he said thoughtfully from the other car.

"Wait a minute! When was this? That you accidentally released a pulse?"

Aurelia felt her cheeks warm. "Um, about a month ago. Why?"

"That was you?" he cried. "I fried my best amp meter! I was working on the ice dragon in my workshop. I thought there was something wrong with the wiring for weeks."

"Sorry," she said, though she wasn't really. It wasn't like Frederick couldn't afford twenty more amp meters from his apprenticeship wages. "But we have a solution to your ice dragon problem now, so you should be thanking me for frying your meter." She smirked, then hopped down from the coal car.

"We need to get to work attaching and hooking up the magnets. That's the last thing I need to do."

"But what about the electromagnetic pulse? The ice? I thought we had agreed to tackle my problem first."

She handed him a crate of her precious magnets, copper wire wrapped around iron tubes, which she would run electricity through in order to create the magnetic fields. When placed opposingly—on the bottom of the locked wheels, and on the track—the electromagnets *should* cause the train to levitate.

"Well lucky for you," she said, "my invention is actually the solution to your problem, once everything is hooked up. And we'll need to move the train out of the barn—I don't want anything exploding in here when we set off the pulse."

"Do you think that's likely?" he said, grunting at the weight of the crate.

"I don't want to chance it. We'll need to hook up the magnets, then the electrical. So it looks like we'll definitely have to come back here tomorrow. You didn't have any Christmas Eve plans, did you?"

"Not since the snow wouldn't stop," he said bitterly.

"Well, we'll solve both our problems now. Finish my train. Stop your storm." She began pointing out where the magnets would go, where she had carefully marked them previously with some red paint. He followed her directions and began bringing the magnets to the designated spots for her to attach.

As she revved the torque gun, her eyes fell on an old paper coffee cup lying on the ground after one of her previous nights of work. "I think I know who we can ask about focusing the pulse beam."

SEVEN

THE DAY BEFORE CHRISTMAS

By some miracle, her boss let them off work two hours early—though, of course, it had less to do with care for his workers than a desire to get home to the delicious meal his wife was making that he had bragged about all day.

A thrill ran through Aurelia as she clocked out, the timeclock stamping her card with a resounding *thud* when she pulled the lever. She was free for a little over a week, until the Dawn of the New Year. And tonight, she and Frederick would hook up her train. The judge would come tomorrow, and one way or another, it would be over.

She pulled the letter from the Magistrate of Invention out of her pocket again, already worn from handling it all day ever since she had gotten it in the post this morning at her workshop. It confirmed her appointment with the judge, at half past nine on Christmas morning. She still couldn't believe they were working on Christmas Day. It was just about the most inconvenient day to get anything done—not to mention ruining any holiday plans people might have.

The city had managed to clear the roads a little better today for the autos, but hadn't bothered with the sidewalks, so Aurelia walked in the street, a cheerful bounce in her step.

She was on her way to meet Frederick at Max's cart. Before her shift this morning, she had told Max she needed to speak with him, and asked where his cart would be when she got out of work. Since she had left the foundry two hours early, she hoped she could still find Max's cart and not waste the extra time she had been given. At least, she knew where he would be two hours from now.

By some luck, Frederick was already waiting at the corner of Solastra Street and Anville Lane where they had agreed. He was leaning against a black wrought-iron lamppost, reading a folded newspaper. Perhaps he had gotten out of work early too.

It was unusual spending so much time with him after

their years apart. He had even bought her a cup of Max's coffee this morning while they had made the plans to meet this afternoon.

He didn't look ruffled in the slightest since she last saw him, after his day apprenticing down at Penydarren Place, the most well-known workshop full of Soldark's leading inventors. He wore a gaudy red and green brocade waistcoat today, with the chain of a watch dangling from one pocket. A black bowler cap protected his hair from the snow, and he had a cup of coffee in his hand. His eyes glinted at her from under the brim of his bowler cap as she trudged through the dirty and uneven snow at the side of the road.

She was glad for the cold for once, the hat and scarf hiding her rumpled hair and sweaty clothes after a long day of work. With how busy she'd been, she hadn't even had a chance to wash her clothes for a few days. *Well, I can take a nice long bath tomorrow as a treat*, she told herself. That is, if they hadn't blown out the electricity in all of Soldark and on the chance that her parents had enough heating gas to spare.

The enticingly warm scent of Frederick's coffee wafted toward her, and she wondered where he had gotten it.

"You're early," she said, finally reaching the corner.

An auto blew by them, somewhat out of control on

the still icy roads. Frederick pulled her out of the way.

"Oh!" she yelped, the auto careening behind her as Frederick pulled her close to his chest.

A hot sensation, then cold, seeped down her pant leg. She backed away and looked down to see his coffee had spilled on both of them.

"Oh no," Frederick said, his hands raised helplessly. "I'm so sorry! Are you all right?"

"Yes, yes, I'm fine. Thank you for that. Not for spilling coffee on me—the other thing."

"Of course," he replied.

"Where'd you get the coffee anyway?" She glanced down at the wet stain and shrugged; she didn't have anything to wipe it dry with anyway.

"Max's," he said. "You know, I've never really talked to him much before. He's a keen fellow."

"You found his cart already?"

He nodded, peering into his coffee cup and finding he still had some left. "My boss gave us a half day. So I wandered around the area to see if I could find him. He's just down at Coppersdown Square right now."

"Well, let's go then. Did you take your auto?" She started walking and he followed. Her boots crunched through the gritty snow still left on the street as they walked along the side. Aurelia kept her ears peeled for any more approaching autos.

"I left it parked at the square," he said. "We can drive to the farm right after. That is, if that's all right with you."

She nodded. A cramped auto ride cooped up with him would be better than taking the train at least.

Coppersdown Square was filled with people and more filled with holiday cheer. Tents and carts had been brought in by vendors like Max, selling food, gifts, and knick-knacks for the last-minute holiday shoppers.

The square was surrounded by four clock towers, one at each corner, each telling a different figure. One told the time, another the temperature, another the date, and the fourth had something to do with astrology—Aurelia didn't really know what that one was.

A covered walkway ran around the edge, filled with vendors who didn't have a tent or anything to cover their goods from the persistent snow, Aurelia suspected. They had tables laid out with metal figurines, pocket watches, jewelry, and plenty of food. The smell of sweet cinnamon and clove assailed her nose, and she wondered where it was coming from.

Max's cart was right under the tower that told the temperature. Aurelia shuddered as she read the pearlescent clock face. Never in her life had she seen the temperature this low.

Max was in his element. He had rigged up a second

urn on the other corner of the cart, and he was filling up cups of coffee left and right. His line wove in front of several other vendors.

Aurelia's face fell. Maybe they would have to wait until later when they were originally supposed to meet Max to even speak with him. He couldn't possibly have time to explain what she needed to know. A selfish thought of taking the time to explore the holiday market passed through Aurelia's head, but she pushed it aside. She had so much work to do.

If they didn't stop the snow soon, the regular trains might stop running. She knew the city was doing their best to try and clear the snow from the train tracks, but the ones leading out into the countryside probably weren't a priority. And soon, there would be nowhere to put the snow they managed to clear from the roads, and no one would be able to drive their autos anywhere. With Aurelia's luck, the judge wouldn't even make it out to the farm. They had to stop this infernal snow.

The newscart operator waved Aurelia over when he spotted her in the crowd. She came over and lifted a gloved hand in greeting.

"Hey," Max said, his face alight at all the excitement. He shifted his newsie cap to let some cool air hit his short-cropped hair. "Isn't this great? Really get a feel for the

Christmas spirit," he said, grinning as he handed someone two cups of coffee.

"I'm sorry we're early," Aurelia said. "We'll just meet you later like we planned."

Max waved her words aside and reached behind him after taking his next customer's order. He handed her a sheet of paper that had more than one coffee stain on it, among the notes and drawings he had done. "I don't know why you're interested in how the coffee urn detects movement with a focused beam, but I'm happy to help with your invention. I had some downtime before I brought the cart to the square." He grinned and handed her a cup of coffee with a wink. "On the house. Merry Christmas, Aurelia."

"Merry Christmas to you too," she said, her face lighting up in a grin as she clutched the paper to her chest. "And thank you! I'll let you know how it all goes!"

He cheerfully waved her off, and she got out of the way of his paying customers. She clutched the notes and coffee as she walked back to where Frederick stood beside an old-fashioned candlemaker's stand.

She eyed the candles for a second as she walked over, thinking her mother would love them. The pretty colored wax poured into unique glass containers was exactly something her mother would like. But she didn't go over for a closer look. Even assuming Frederick might drive her out to the farm tomorrow, too, she didn't have enough coppers for anything like that.

"He made us some notes," she told Frederick, holding up the paper.

"Perfect. We can get a head start. I parked my auto just around the block."

Aurelia sipped her coffee as they walked to the auto and was surprised to taste a hint of cinnamon and clove. It was delicious and warmed her like nothing else.

Frederick opened the passenger door for her, and she gave him a look before getting in.

"What?" he asked when he got in the driver's seat.

"Nothing. Do you have everything you need to hook up the electrical this time?"

"Yes," he said, "I loaded everything up this morning. We'll be pulling off the Grandville Electric grid, but I don't think anyone will notice. And if they do, I'll put it under my account."

He started the auto with a chugging roar and pulled out onto the icy road.

"Be careful," Aurelia warned him, clutching her coffee to keep it from spilling as he pulled the auto into the next lane. "No one seems to want to drive slowly in this mess."

"It's not as if I've ever driven in snow before," he said.

"It's the first time Soldark's had snow in a hundred years, remember?"

She scoffed. "Yes, and I think I remember why. Something to do with an overly ambitious inventor going way too far with an invention he didn't even need to make."

"I wouldn't say I'm *overly* ambitious. Perhaps just the normal amount. And what do you mean an invention I didn't need to make? Who really needs a reason to invent something?"

She took a sip of her coffee, regretting bringing it up. The cinnamon and clove wove through her senses on the way down. "Well, you don't really need to enter this competition, do you? You'll get into the inventor's union soon enough on your own merits, what with your position at Penydarren Place and all."

Frederick didn't say anything for a few minutes as they drove out of city limits. "People keep saying that, but I haven't done anything to draw the eye of the master inventors, no matter how hard I try. I'll never get enough notoriety to join the union at this rate. I think they just like having cheap apprentices around to do their busy work. You were better off striking out on your own."

She turned to look at him incredulously. "I didn't strike out on my own because I *wanted to*, I was up for that same apprenticeship you don't even value!

Remember?"

"Not really," he admitted, his hands sliding to a different position on the steering wheel. "I didn't know you were in the running at the time. When I found out after... I mean, I felt bad that you didn't get it, but you don't really resent me for winning it, do you? Is that why you haven't spoken to me in seven years? You're upset about *that*?"

She flumped back into the seat, her coffee almost gone already. She looked down into the cup and said, "That's not it, and you know it."

The ride turned even bumpier as they reached the country lane leading past the Morrisons' farm, and soon after, her parents' fields. She looked out the windows at the dead crops and didn't say anything further. She finished her coffee, the dregs bitter. She felt slightly ill after not eating for a few hours, but the coffee had been worth it.

When they got closer to the house, Aurelia saw an auto pulled up in front again. *Not again.* Her heart dropped to her stomach. This couldn't be good news.

She didn't say anything when Frederick put his auto in park, just ripped open the latch and bolted from the car. She shoved her way through the thick snowdrifts as fast as she could up to the porch, then ran inside the house.

"Father?" she called, her hand on the banister at the bottom of the stairs. Her heart was thudding. Was it the doctor's auto? Had something happened?

Her father appeared at the top of the stairs, with her mother leaning on his arm. Aurelia couldn't repress the sigh of relief at the wonderful sight of her mother out of bed. The doctor was just behind them as they all came down the creaking stairs.

Aurelia heard Frederick silently enter the house, then wander into the sitting room out of the way.

"Mother," she said, "you're looking so well. Should you be out of bed?"

"Do you think Doctor Abbeysworth would be letting me if I shouldn't?" her mother replied with a smile. She looked thinner and paler than usual, but her face was glowing with health. She was wearing her holiday nightgown, embroidered at the ends of the long white sleeves and hem with holly leaves and berries.

Aurelia pulled her mother into a one-armed hug when she reached the bottom. She smiled at her father and the doctor, not sure what to say. She never felt comfortable talking about her mother's health in front of her.

The doctor saved her from asking what she wanted to know. "The new medication is working wonders for your mother," she said, closing up the handles of her black leather bag with a *snap*. She adjusted the cravat at her throat then checked her pocket watch. "Sometimes these things just need adjusting. Well, good luck tomorrow, Aurelia; your parents told me all about your invention."

Warmth spread to her cheeks and Aurelia said, "Thank you Doctor Abbeysworth. And thank you for taking care of my mother." She stuck her hand out to shake, and the doctor bid them farewell and went out into the snowy night.

Her mother smiled at her, then glanced into the sitting room where Frederick stood by the fire, adeptly staying out of the family discussion. "The doctor said it might not even have been the cold, since it's still so cold and I'm feeling better already."

"That's great," Aurelia replied truthfully. She would never, *ever*, forgive Frederick if something terrible had happened to her mother because of his idiotic invention. The crops were bad enough.

"Is that Frederick Grandville?" her mother asked. "You know, your father and I haven't had dinner yet. We could all sit down together for a Christmas Eve dinner. Wouldn't that be nice?"

Aurelia's face crumpled. "I'd love to, Mother, truly, but Frederick and I have a lot of work to do tonight on the train. The judge is coming at nine-thirty tomorrow morning."

And she wasn't really sure she wanted to sit down to dinner with just Frederick and her parents. It screamed of an intimacy they no longer had, and she was still seething from their conversation on the way over. How could he not remember what had driven them apart. The promise he had broken.

"Well, you get to work then," her mother said, chucking her on the shoulder. I'll send your father out with some turkey sandwiches when it's done roasting."

"Thanks," Aurelia said, unable to keep from smiling. "Frederick, let's get out to the barn while there's still a little light out."

With a few polite words to her parents, Frederick followed her outside. It was slow going through the ever-increasing snow, and Aurelia was glad to get into the barn where she stomped off her boots.

Frederick rigged up a control panel and began running a line to the Grandville Electric box out by the Soldark Line tracks, just a little farther off from the abandoned track. He came in and out of the barn a few times while Aurelia finished up modifications on the train.

She was again glad she had already installed the magnets on the train tracks a while back; there was no way she could get to them easily now. Her fingers were already half-frozen as she finally finished. She flexed her hands inside her leather gloves to try and warm them.

The wheels were locked, the magnets in place, cables run to each. Now all she needed was the power to charge them. Once the current was live, the magnetic field generated by each electromagnet would create enough lift to levitate the train. Then, the magnets installed in the tracks would help push and pull it forward depending on the polarity of the magnets.

That was the idea anyway. She just hoped all of her calculations were correct, and the magnetic fields were large enough to lift the heavy antique. She had gutted plenty of unneeded parts and sold them for scrap, but the construction of the train was quite solid.

She sat down on an empty crate and pulled out her headlamp and Max's notes to study.

Finally, Frederick came back in, and he clapped his hands. "It should be ready," he told her. "Let me just check the readings down on this end before I flip the switch."

He brought a handheld meter to the control panel he'd set up on a stack of crates just inside the barn door. Wires snaked from the brass box, while switches, buttons, and knobs decorated the top. He checked a few wires with his meter and turned to Aurelia who had just come up behind him. "I think we're ready. Any progress on the focusing beam?"

"Yes," she said, pointing to part of Max's diagram. "See here where the detection beam connects to the urn? The beam isn't the same as what we need to do, but the theory helps. See how he did the wiring?"

"Oh," Frederick said, leaning in close. "But how will we use the train to generate the pulse beam?"

"The train will act as the transformer since it's going to have the power running through it and the magnets, but we'll need to add a set of antennas on top, and a couple of capacitors to focus the magnetic field into a beam shape."

They got to work. Frederick brought out a few wind-up lights much like Aurelia's headlamp, but these looked more like old-fashioned lanterns, which he placed on the top of the train car where they would be working. Aurelia's father brought them some turkey sandwiches with cranberry jam, and some hot chocolate.

Aurelia was itching to turn on the electricity and try the mag-train out, but there would be time enough for that once they finished the focusing beam. She certainly didn't want to have to get up on top of the train outside in the snow to rig everything up. So they stayed in the barn and finished the adjustments. Once the electromagnetic pulse generator was all set, they could move the train out and aim it at the sky, where the clockwork ice dragon circled Soldark.

Straddling the train car, an almond cookie in her mouth as she fiddled with the three antennas, Aurelia nearly jumped out of her skin at a roaring sound from above.

She looked up at the barn's ceiling, wondering if the clockwork dragon was somehow already falling down upon them. But no, glancing at the side of the barn, she could see through the gaps in the planks that snow was falling in an avalanche from the roof.

"Wow," Frederick said, glancing up at her, pliers in hand.

"I know," she said around the last bite of her cookie. "Hey, I think I'm done with the antennas. How about you?"

"Done."

"Ready to power it up?" she asked, grinning. She couldn't wait to flip the switch and turn on her train after all the planning and accumulating parts with her measly wages. Her ticket into the union.

"I guess."

"You guess?" she asked incredulously. "We're done! We'll bring down the clockwork ice dragon, no one will be the wiser, and my train will work just in time. What's the matter with you?"

"I just..." He put down the pliers and looked her right in the eyes. "What you said earlier. About us. The reason you stopped wanting to see me. I feel as if I did something wrong."

Aurelia's chest burned, first in anger. *How could he possibly forget? He doesn't even know what he did?*

And then her cheeks flamed in embarrassment. *He doesn't remember. Had she misinterpreted what had happened? Had she been holding a grudge for all these years for nothing?*

"I—You—" She huffed, her breath coming out in a cloud between them. "You promised me something, and you went back on that promise."

He frowned. "What promise?"

"I don't really want to talk about this. Can we just turn on the train?" she pleaded.

Scooting closer, down the top of the train car, he shook his head. "What promise?"

She looked up at the ceiling, as if the right words might be up there somewhere, might fall on her like an avalanche of snow. "Fine. You promised you'd never make me feel bad about being—well, poor, when we were dating. And on your eighteenth birthday, you held a party at your parents' estate."

"Right..." he said, clearly not remembering what had happened.

"And I came and met your parents and friends from home and more family, your cousins…" she paused, hoping he might jump in and stop her. But unfortunately, she had to continue to explain the scene that had repeated in her head for seven years, whenever she felt down about herself.

She didn't look at him.

"Well, once I was alone, two of your cousins cornered me in the back gardens. One of them kicked me down to the ground, and the other shoved mud in my face. They told me you didn't want me there, that you were embarrassed I had even come." She lowered her voice in mortification. "It was a formal event, remember? And you know I've never owned formal clothes in my entire life. Then I had to run all the way home."

She felt a hand on her chin, and she looked up, startled. She hadn't heard him come any closer.

"I never knew about that," he said. "I swear. I never even *thought* those words about you. And I certainly didn't say anything of the sort to my cousins."

Her chest swelled, but she was not about to start crying. The tears might freeze to her face.

He cocked his head. "I always wondered why you left early that night. I had been meaning to give you a gift, and then I never saw you again, never heard back when I tried to send you telegrams or letters even."

Flashes of torn up letters and telegrams flew threw her mind, along with the memory of dumping a whole box of them into the fire, unopened.

Another roaring sound from above intruded. Aurelia looked around to see where the snow was sliding, and then she saw movement outside the open barn doors. The snow was coming off the front of the house now, dropping straight onto Frederick's auto, which was parked outside the front door.

She gasped, and Frederick turned to see his auto buried in several days' accumulation.

Aurelia took the distraction to slide over the side of the train car and lower herself down, wedging her boots into crevices and grabbing rods and bolts for handholds until she got back down to the ground. She wandered over to the doorway to get a better look at the buried auto. It was getting harder to see the house from here; the snow was coming down thick and fast.

Frederick wasn't far behind her. "Ah, oh well. We can worry about that later." He shrugged.

Aurelia went over to the electric control panel Frederick had set up, still not looking at him. Since he had been the one to configure the panel, she wasn't sure what everything did yet. Her finger hovered over a switch she thought might be the one to turn on the power to everything.

"Wait, Aurelia," he said from behind her. She didn't turn. "I'm sorry my cousins did that to you back then—and I really had no idea. I didn't know what I did wrong. And then the next year I heard I beat you out of the apprenticeship, and I... I guess I've chalked it up to that this whole time."

Her voice was a little wobbly when she said, "Well, the apprenticeship situation didn't help matters. Can we just do this?"

"I want—" he began.

A screeching noise met their ears. This wasn't more snow falling from roofs. It was coming from much higher up.

Aurelia darted just outside the door, gazing up at the clouds. It seemed like it was coming from up there. "The clockwork dragon," she breathed. "Is that it? What in the republic is that noise?"

"I've no idea," Frederick replied beside her. "It sounds mechanical. I wonder if something's jammed. There certainly seems to be a lot more snow than before," he said loudly. Between the wind and the screeching, it was getting hard to hear anything else.

"Quick, let's turn the beam on," he said.

"No, we have to pull the train out first. I'm not risking

anything happening to the barn, and it'll have a clearer shot out in the open."

"All right."

They rushed back to the control panel, and Frederick's finger went to the big brass lever at the bottom right. Then he said, "Do you want to do the honors?"

She grinned and stepped forward. "Absolutely." She clutched the lever and flipped on the power.

A loud hum came from the train, filling the barn with even more noise than what was going on outside.

"Is it working?" she asked, almost afraid to go and see.

He said nothing, only pointed.

She ran over to inspect it. The wheels, locked in place and their electromagnets firmly bolted to the bottoms, were hovering nearly a foot off the track. "Wow," she whispered. "I didn't think it would go that high. That's...incredible. Did you send more power to it than I had in my calculations?"

Frederick came over with a mischievous grin. "I might have."

"What?" she yelped, lurching backward. "You could have fried everything! I calculated the exact amount we needed—I've tested it small-scale dozens of times."

For a minute they both just stared at the gap between the wheels and the track, a wonder of electromagnetic energy that had seemed almost impossible. Like magic, if there was such a thing.

"It looks good to me," Frederick said.

"Well, I'll let you get in it first and see if you get electrocuted. Now I don't know if I can trust your wiring."

He continued grinning and reached out to touch the handrail. He grasped it firmly, then pulled himself up and into the cab. "Aren't you coming on for the first voyage?"

She followed him in, hurling herself upward into the cab, now a foot higher than it was before. She couldn't tell if she was imagining the feeling of floating as she planted her boots on the cab floor. He moved aside so she could get to the conductor's control panel.

"Here we go," she said, her heart racing as she pushed the lever forward that would direct the magnets' poles to begin pulling the train from the front and pushing from the back.

The movement was smooth, unlike anything she had ever experienced on the Soldark Line's steam trains.

They began to glide forward, but when they reached the barn door opening, where snow was piled upon the track, they slowed to a stop.

EIGHT

N o!" Aurelia shouted, slamming her fist on the side of the cab. Without any clear thought, she shoved past Frederick and swung herself down and out. She stared at the front of the train.

The snow was much too high. Even a foot off the ground was not enough, and for all she knew, the accumulation was interfering with the magnetic fields. She came around the front, sinking into the cold snowdrifts. Then she had an idea.

"Back it up a bit!" she called to Frederick, who had remained in the cab, his face frozen, unsure what to do next. "Pull the lever back."

She raced over to her toolbox and pulled out her torque gun. "Now come give me a hand! This is going to be heavy."

Revving the torque gun, she unbolted the large pilot mounted at the front of the train, its pointed front designed to deflect obstacles in front of it down the track. But now the track was much lower, and the pilot wasn't able to clear anything from up so high.

They both grunted at the weight of the pilot as it came loose. Aurelia turned to grab her headlamp from a nearby crate and jammed it on her head, glad it still had a charge. She stared at the front of the train, looking for places to re-mount it. She gazed into the guts of the train, not sure if this would work or not.

"There!" Frederick said, pointing. "And along there! Here—" He lifted the pilot and got it close to where they could mount it, low enough to plow aside the snow.

Aurelia used one hand to help line up the pilot with the bolt holes, and the other hand to rev up her torque gun, bolting the thing in place while Frederick held it up. The sound of the torque gun drowned out the screeching from outside, and the howling of the storm.

Finally, they got it in place, about a foot lower from where it started. She and Frederick looked at each other, their eyes wide in excitement. Without a word, they both headed back into the cab, and Aurelia jammed the lever forward.

They glided into motion, gathering speed as they went. The pilot plowed the snow aside, clearing the track as they went. It was difficult to pull back on the lever to slow down—not because anything was wrong with it, but because she wanted to keep racing down the track. She could try *that* later, when they had stopped the clockwork ice dragon and stopped the snow from burying them here out in the middle of the countryside.

The train emerged into the open field before it. Aurelia and Frederick were pelted with snow coming in from the side of the conductor's cab. The screeching above had turned into a keening whine coming from the clouds, and the white flakes were still coming down thick and fast.

Reaching the middle of the field, a good distance from both the house and barn, Aurelia pulled the lever all the way back. Slowly, the magnetic poles allowed it to stop.

"All right," she said, a little breathless. "Are you ready to generate the pulse?"

Frederick nodded. "And you're sure it won't power down the train or fry it?" he asked.

"The pulse will focus in a beam, upwards. And I'm pretty sure we'll get the clockwork dragon—it feels like it's right above us."

"Wait a minute," Frederick said. "It's just going to fall out of the sky, right?"

Aurelia's jaw fell, and she closed her mouth. "What if it falls on the house? What if it's not even near here and kills some unsuspecting people?"

Frederick slapped a hand to his forehead. "Gah! I'm such an idiot for inventing this thing! I can't do anything right!"

"Frederick! Frederick, just stop and think for a moment," she said, grabbing hold of his arms and shaking him a little. "All right, so it's going to fall out of the sky," she said, trying to jumpstart some ideas in either of them. "We need to control the landing. Let's think."

Frederick closed his eyes, thinking hard. "Assuming the pulse doesn't kill the train—"

"Don't you dare say that! The train will be fine. It has to be fine."

"All right, all right. The train will be fine. What if we reverse all the electromagnets after the beam goes off—and pull everything down to the track? How big is the track? How far did you run the magnets?"

Aurelia gasped. "It's not huge—it runs from the barn out and along these two fields, where it used to connect to the old Soldark Line. But the tracks aren't even connected anymore. I ran the magnets as far as I could go. We could! We could do it!"

"Lucky my auto's buried in snow," Frederick said.

"What? Why?"

"Well, when we reverse all the magnets—instead of the flux push and pull pattern you've got running through the track now, it'll pull a lot of metal toward the track, probably even the auto if it weren't buried."

She snorted out a giggle. "Let's do this!"

"Wait," Frederick said, looking down at the controls. "We can generate the pulse beam from here—but your track's master electromagnetic system is rigged up in the barn. I'll have to go back—you generate the pulse, and then I'll flip the magnets, all right?"

"All right," she said, glancing at the distance to the barn, a blizzard crossing the field between. "Don't walk on the tracks, remember? And I'll signal you with my headlamp as soon as I've run the pulse."

"Just be careful, all right?" he said, one hand on the railing as he readied to hop out of the cab. "The clockwork dragon will hopefully get pulled down to the track—but it could be any part of the track. So keep an eye on the sky—you won't be able to move the train."

"Got it," she said, nodding.

"Thank you." He caught her gaze and stared fiercely at her. "For everything. Soldark would be buried without your help."

"It's not over yet, Grandville," she said, her finger on the pulse beam's lever.

He ducked his head. "I know, but we've almost done it. And I'm sorry you ever believed that I thought less of you. I never knew what came between us, and I'm sorry you thought I broke that promise. I would never."

She shivered in the cold cab as a gust of wind pelted her with more snow. Her eyelids fluttered as the flakes assailed her, and suddenly Frederick was standing right in front of her.

"Thank you," he said, and leaned down to kiss her.

Her eyes closed and she shivered again, but not from the cold wind. A warmth began at her lips and spread down to her chest, to her fingertips. She breathed in his scent—so familiar, yet at the same time so foreign. It had been seven years.

Knees beginning to weaken, she kissed him back fiercely, then broke apart. "We've got more pressing matters," she said, pointing up at the sky, where the keening had returned to a loud screeching. "Maybe we'll have more time for that later."

A haphazard grin spreading across his face, he leapt out of the cab and went as fast as he could through the snowdrifts; in some places it rose up to his hips, but others were ankle-high thanks to the wind.

Aurelia licked her lips, just as more snow pelted at her from the cab window, and the taste of winter flicked across her tongue. She took a steadying breath as she watched Frederick get closer to the barn.

"Oh, right," she muttered, then fumbled with her headlamp, still attached to her head. She yanked it off and cranked the reel so it would have more of a charge. By the time Frederick got to the barn, it was ready. She gave him the count of two minutes after he got inside—the control panel was right inside the door; he should have plenty of time to get ready—and then she flipped the lever for the electromagnetic pulse beam.

A hum sounded throughout the train cab, louder than the gentle hum of levitation, louder than the screeching above. The beam was working—running anyway.

Headlamp in hand, she flashed it toward the barn, angling the light back and forth. Then, without warning, the train dropped to the tracks.

She threw her hands out to grab hold of anything to catch her balance at the jarring landing. Her teeth chattered together, not from the cold. Frederick had reversed the polarity.

All that was left to do was wait for the clockwork menace to fall.

She closed her eyes for a second. And just like that, the screeching in the clouds stopped.

Aurelia opened her eyes and went to the open cab

door. Clutching the handlebar, she leaned out of the train and looked up.

Snow whirled around her, the wind still barreling across the open field. She couldn't tell, but it looked like it could be thinning.

And then she heard a whistling sound. Eyes wide, she searched the skies. Where was it? Should she get out of the train? Would she be safer inside it? She would *kill* Frederick if this thing demolished her invention, just when she had gotten it to work.

A cloud drifted away, and she saw it in the newly revealed moonlight. The clockwork ice dragon was falling, sinking and breaking through clouds, snowflakes fluttering in its wake.

And it was heading right for the barn.

NINE

"Frederick!" she shouted, leaping down from the cab, her legs sinking into the snow. She fought her way through the drifts, stumbling, pushing. The beam of her headlamp wove in a drunken pattern across the snowy field as she lurched across.

It was as if all noise had ceased. No humming, no screeching, no howling wind. Just the blessed silence of the last of the snowflakes drifting peacefully down to the earth.

The dark shadow that was the clockwork dragon dropped faster toward the old barn. "Frederick!" she screamed at the top of her lungs, not sure if he could hear her despite the seeming lack of sound. "Frederick!"

She stumbled and fell into a snowdrift. By the time

she clawed her way back out, she looked up in time to see the clockwork dragon crash into the barn.

In the vacuum of silence, the crash filled the frozen world around her. Wooden beams splintering, shattering, crashing. The sound of metal crumpling as it all came apart. It went on and on as pieces of the barn collapsed onto the clockwork contraption that had destroyed it.

She continued trudging toward the barn, as if she moved through cold molasses.

Everything was suddenly and completely still. The snow had stopped, the final flakes settled. The barn, which was now piles of timber, lay like an open wound in the snowy white field. And in the middle of it all, the clockwork ice dragon lay, the canvas stretching over the wings torn, gears and rods sticking out in all directions. Aurelia could see what looked like the head of the dragon sticking up, steam issuing from its open mouth as it breathed its last.

"Frederick," she mumbled, her lips numb with cold. Her legs, just as numb, could barely make it through the last of the snow.

She sunk down to her knees when she saw him, not even feeling the cold wetness pressing through her trousers. He was kneeling beside the clockwork dragon, hand stroking the face of it, talking to himself—or it.

"Frederick!" she shouted, getting to her feet again. "You're all right!"

He turned, a sheepish grin on his face as he dropped his hand from the face of the dragon.

"I didn't see you leave the barn! How are you all right?"

"I thought I should get away from the track, so I got out right after I flipped the polarity."

She puffed out a breath and closed her eyes for a second, the adrenaline washing out of her.

He took one last look at the broken dragon, still issuing steam from its mouth, then turned and enveloped her in a hug. He smelled of the cold, and electricity, and a familiar scent she couldn't place.

He pulled away and looked at her, cradling her face in his gloved hands. "We did it! We did it!" He leaned his forehead against hers, and she closed her eyes, suddenly exhausted.

The last hour or so had been a terrible mess of storm, and sound, and terror. When she looked up, he opened his eyes, too, and their lips met as one final snowflake drifted down from the heavens.

TEN

CHRISTMAS DAY

At nine-thirty the next morning, Aurelia stood at the front porch of her parents' house, watching the judge approach down the lane in his auto.

The sun was shining again.

The snow that had covered Frederick's auto had been cleared, and both the auto and Frederick were gone before Aurelia even woke up. He had accepted Aurelia's father's offer to sleep on the settee in the sitting room, and Aurelia had collapsed into her bed upstairs well past midnight, fully clothed. She had managed to shuck off her soaking wet boots, at least.

With no idea where Frederick had gone, Aurelia had tromped out to what used to be the barn that morning to check on the train. She had woken before sunup with a terrible thought—what had happened to the control panel inside the barn? Lurching out of bed, she had jammed her boots on and hurried downstairs and outside.

After fiddling with the levers, she realized the control panel was still intact. But she also suspected that Frederick had been out here before she awoke, since planks had been shifted aside, and fresh shoe prints had led to the panel. And she noticed that the pulse beam antenna had been removed from the train too.

She had barely glanced at the ruins of the clockwork ice dragon before heading over to the train. After making sure that that, too, was operational, she went back inside the house and had a surprisingly normal breakfast with her parents. They chatted over coffee and cinnamon rolls as Aurelia anxiously waited for nine-thirty.

And now, here came the judge. His auto was even more expensive-looking than Frederick's. An older gentleman stepped from the passenger seat, putting on a top hat and pulling out a cane with an emerald topper. The driver, a boy Aurelia's age, remained in the auto.

"Leland Cornwall," the gentleman said, holding out his hand to her.

She shook it, reminding herself to keep her grip firm. "Aurelia Sundon. It's nice to meet you, Mr. Cornwall. Thank you for coming out all this way and on Christmas."

"Of course, of course. Not as if I had a choice. The Office of the Magistrate pulls all the strings, my dear. So here I am." He shrugged.

She smiled, immediately liking the older man. He had a monocle perched in one eye, and the red and green cravat at his throat was tasteful and not gaudy for the holiday.

"Let me bring you around to where my invention is," she said, "but first, would you like any coffee? Tea? Cinnamon rolls?"

"No, thank you. That's quite kind. I've four more stops to make today unless you're the clear winner. I've, at least, got the authority to induct any inventors I see fit, even if I didn't get to make up any of the rules for this competition."

A shiver ran through her, and for once it had nothing to do with the cold. She was so close, she could taste it. She relished the sunshine that shone down upon them as she led him behind the house to where she had left the train. The paths they had worn to and from the barn were becoming slushy and muddy.

"Marvelous," Cornwall said in awe as they rounded the corner. The train was levitating a foot off the track, looking for all the world as if she had done magic to it instead of all the careful scientific calculations. Or at least, that's how she thought of it. She had decided to turn everything on before the judge arrived, just for this purpose.

"Let me show you how it moves," she said, and sprung toward the conductor's cab. She launched herself up into the high cab and readied herself in front of the controls. Peeking her head out of the cab window, she saw Cornwall pull a small notebook from his coat pocket and begin writing in it.

She waited until he looked up before she moved the lever. Slowly at first, the train began to move down the track toward the barn, the pushing and pulling of the electromagnets levitating her along.

"Wonderful!" Cornwall called. She could hear him chuckling as she passed him, and the smile grew wider on her face. She had it. It was in the bag.

But as she approached the barn, she heard the sound of clanking metal, and then—astonishingly—wheels creaking. *Was something wrong with the train?* She hadn't felt it drop down to the tracks.

Then she looked out the window and saw a large truck and crane approaching down the side of the field toward the ruins of the barn. *What was going on?*

She pulled the lever back and slowed down the train, sure the demonstration had been enough to impress Cornwall.

When she hopped down, Cornwall wasn't even looking at his notepad, merely staring at the train.

"So what do you think?" she couldn't help but ask.

"Well done, Ms. Sundon! Why, I think—"

The crane and truck were close now, their mechanical jangling loud as they approached the barn.

Much to her surprise, Frederick came out of the passenger side of the truck when it parked.

"I'm so sorry," she told Cornwall. "Would you excuse me for a moment?"

He waved her away, "Not at all, not at all. I'd like to get a closer look inside—may I?"

"Please," she said, and lent her arm to help him up into the high cab.

She strode over to Frederick and hissed, "What are you doing? The judge is here!"

"I'm sorry," he said, glancing back at where Cornwall stood inside the train cab, investigating the control panel. "I tried to get them here before the judge arrived to clean this mess up. But you have no idea how hard it was to convince them I was serious."

"Well, it's Christmas Day, you dolt. Did you pull them away from their families?"

"What? No, of course not. No, they were on duty already. They just didn't think I meant I wanted to clean up a whole barn in one morning, plus haul out a large piece of machinery, on today of all days."

The two men who had come with the truck and crane were now staring at the piece of machinery in question, the remains of the clockwork dragon. A limp and broken wing stuck up from the pile, gears sprawled across the planks of wood, the head visible even from where Aurelia stood. And then she noticed Frederick must have moved the pulse beam antenna from the train over near the dragon; it leaned against its damaged chest.

"Ah, Mr. Grandville," Cornwall said as he joined them. "I'm scheduled to judge your invention at four this evening. I don't suppose—"

Frederick smiled and shook Cornwall's hand as if he already knew him well. Frederick glanced at Aurelia and then at the dragon. Her stomach lurched. *He wasn't going to steal her judge, now, was he? She was this close!*

His dragon was in ruins, but he had moved the pulse beam antenna over here...

"Looks like you'll finish with your judging early today, then," Frederick told him. "I'm out of the running. Behind me is the failure that was my invention."

Aurelia's heart fluttered and she let out a breath.

"Oh, my dear boy, my judging today is done already. I have my clear selection right here," Cornwall said, and clapped a hand on Aurelia's shoulder.

For a second, she didn't register the words.

Then her eyes bulged. "Really? Really?"

"Yes, really," Cornwall said, adjusting his monocle as he peered back to where her train still levitated off the humming tracks. "That is the most innovative invention I've seen in a very long time. Now I can go back to the Magistrate of Invention and tell them doing this on Christmas was an abomination of protocol." He lowered his voice, "The union reps forced a vote that we open up a contest this year for anyone in Soldark, and the higher-ups wanted to weed out sub-par inventors from applying. They seemed to think a last-minute Christmas deadline would result in fewer applicants."

Aurelia stifled a gasp. *So that was why.*

"When I tell them what you have here," Cornwall continued, "They'll regret looking down on candidates who don't show the 'right' career path or what have you."

She glanced at Frederick. The surprise at this information was evident on his face too.

"Well, congratulations," Cornwall said, shaking her hand again. "Welcome to the inventor's union, Ms. Sundon. I'll send along a courier with your prize money this afternoon, and all of the glorious paperwork we need you to fill out. Once you've joined the union, you'll have all kinds of opportunities. Just don't apply for management," he added in a stage whisper. "They make you work on Christmas."

A giggle burst from her throat, and she wanted to fling her arms around the old man and hug him, but she instead offered him coffee again, or more time to look at the train.

He shook his head and straightened his top hat before making his way back to his auto. Before he rounded the corner of the house he called out, "If you need anyone to consult on getting patents for your marvelous invention, please, get in touch, Ms. Sundon. I'd love to see more of your inventions."

"I will!" she called, raising a hand in farewell.

She was grinning from ear to ear when she turned back to Frederick, who was watching the two workers make a plan for the barn cleanup.

"You didn't have to do this," she said, wondering how much it cost to rent a crane and hire the men to operate it.

"I kind of did," he replied. "Soldark would be buried in snow without you. The least I can do is replace your family's barn. Besides, I need to get my clockwork dragon back to my workshop."

"You're not going to—"

"No, no. Never again will I meddle with the weather. And besides, it was fried, remember? I just want to scrap the parts."

"Good," she said.

He slipped his hand into hers, and she felt a small box there when he pulled away.

"What's this?"

"For you. Merry Christmas."

"Oh, Frederick, you didn't have to—when did you even—"

Her protests were interrupted when his lips met hers. They were warm and sweet and tasted of ginger.

"I've wanted to give that to you for a long time," he said. "Go ahead."

She pulled the lid off the small nondescript brown box. Inside were a pair of earrings. But not just any earrings. "The dragon earrings!" She gasped. "From the Fawney Fair we went to the last summer of school! How do you even have these?"

He shrugged and tucked his hands into his waistcoat pockets. He'd done away with the gaudy red and green, and today was wearing a more mellow brown and gold waistcoat to match his brown pants and bowler cap. "I told you, I've had it for a long time. I was going to give them to you that night...of the party," he ended awkwardly.

"Oh," she said, poking a finger into the small box and touching the earrings amid the wood shaving padding. Made of real silver with actual emeralds for eyes, the dragons hung from the earring posts by their claws, their wings spreading wide, and tails curling down at the bottom. She had thought they were marvelous that day at the fair with Frederick. But she had never been able to afford anything like them in her life.

Frederick cleared his throat, and she looked up. "They were kind of the inspiration for..." He nodded to the clockwork dragon.

"No," she said. "Really? But why the snow?"

"Well... Don't laugh, but I... wanted to impress you. You know I rented that workshop space in your building to try and speak to you again."

She shifted on her feet and glanced back down at the dragon earrings. She had wondered why he had rented a space in that part of town, when he could easily have a workspace at home in his father's estate.

"I... don't know what to say," she admitted.

"Say you like the earrings? Say you'll come back to my house for Christmas dinner?"

She chuckled. "I have grand plans today, Frederick. They involve a bath, and filling my face with as much Christmas dinner as I possibly can, and celebrating with my parents about the prize the train has won us."

"Well, I could help with the dinner part," he said, "but I'll leave you to your grand plans here. I was planning on riding back with the clockwork dragon once they've extricated it. I'll have builders out here as soon as the ground looks good enough to pour new foundation posts. It's a mix of ice and mud at the moment," he said, looking down at his shiny brown shoes that were covered in mud and slush.

"Thank you," she said, pulling him into a hug as she slipped the earrings into her pocket. "For the barn, for everything—well, no, not for almost ruining my invention and dumping all that snow on us, but, you know."

He smirked. "I guess I got your attention with the dragon after all."

She punched him lightly on the shoulder. "Never go to those lengths again to get anyone's attention. Your ideas are dangerous."

A grin lit up his face. "Well, as long as I have you to save me from myself..." he murmured, pulling her back into his arms.

"Within reason," she agreed.

THE END

ALSO BY LIZ DELTON

Seasons of Soldark
Spectacle of the Spring Queen
The Mechanical Masquerade
All Hallows Airship
The Clockwork Ice Dragon

Everturn Chronicles
The Alchemyst's Mirror

The Realm of Camellia Series
The Starless Girl
The Storm King
The Gray Mage
The Starlight Dragon
The Rogue Shadow

The Four Cities of Arcera
Meadowcity
The Fifth City
A Rift Between Cities
Sylvia in the Wilds

Notebooks for Writers

Writer's Notebook
Teen Writer's Notebook
Guided Writer's Notebook
Writer's Planner

ABOUT THE AUTHOR

Liz Delton writes and lives in New England, with her husband and sons. She studied Theater Management at the University of the Arts in Philly, always having enjoyed the backstage life of storytelling.

She reads and writes fantasy, especially the kind with alternate worlds. World-building is her favorite part of writing, and she is always dreaming up new fantastic places.

She loves drinking tea and traveling. When she's not writing you can find her hands full with one of her many craft projects.

Visit her website at **LizDelton.com**

Made in the USA
Middletown, DE
29 June 2024

56496763R00064